SLEEPING BEAUTY

Sarah Gibb

Once upon a time there lived a king and queen who had almost everything they could possibly wish for. But neither was content, for there was one thing missing… they both wanted a child.

One day the Queen saw a rosebud floating in the fountain and it smelled so sweet, she put her hand in to pull it out. Just then, a bright green frog leaped out of the water and spoke to her.

"Don't be afraid," he said. "I have good news for you. Before long you will have a baby girl." And he jumped back into the water with a tiny splash.

The Queen was overjoyed and ran straight indoors to tell the King what had happened.

The following spring just, as the frog had promised, a beautiful little girl was born and the palace bustled with joy. The King and Queen were so delighted that they decided to celebrate with a magnificent party.

"Everyone in the kingdom will be invited," said the King, beaming with pride.

In those days it was the custom when a royal baby was born to send out invitations to all the fairies in the realm, from the tiniest to the most powerful. Messengers were sent out all over the land.

But one fairy, who had not been seen for more than fifty years, was forgotten. And she was the oldest and most powerful of all. Her name was Malevola.

"So, they don't want *me* at the party?" she snarled. "Well, let's see if they like my gift!"

On the day of the party, the King and Queen welcomed the
fairies as they arrived, and led them all into a beautiful hall full
of flowers.

"The Princess's name is Rosebud," announced the King as
the fairies came forward to give their magical gifts.

"Then she will be as beautiful as a rose," said the first fairy.

"Everyone will love her," said another.

"She will be very clever," promised a third.

"…kind…"

"…graceful…"

"…lucky in love…"

As they went on the Queen began to lose count of the wonderful gifts being showered upon little Rosebud, sleeping sweetly in her arms.

All of a sudden the air grew freezing cold, and at the entrance to the hall was Malevola hidden in shadow.

"You didn't ask me to the party, but I've come anyway!" she cried. "And here is my gift… Beautiful and clever she may be, but when she is sixteen, the Princess will prick her finger on a spindle and die!"

The other fairies shrieked with horror, and the Queen held her precious baby close. But Malevola had already disappeared into the night.

Just then a tiny fairy with a wand that shone like pink fire flew out of the shadows and hovered above the little Princess. "I haven't given *my* gift," she said.

The Queen lifted her baby up to the fairy.

"When you prick your finger, you shall not die, Rosebud," said the fairy. "You will fall into a deep sleep until a hundred years have passed, when a prince will wake you."

The King and Queen wept as the fairies said goodbye. What a terrible future for their little princess.

The next day the King was determined to beat the evil spell and ordered that every spindle in his kingdom was to be burned on a huge fire.

The little fairy, who had stayed behind to keep watch over the Princess, shook her head and whispered, "What's done cannot so easily be undone!"

Years passed and the King and Queen began to believe that they had outwitted Malevola.

Rosebud grew as beautiful, clever and kind as the fairies had promised. She was as graceful as a deer and so loving that no one ever wished her a moment's harm.

But the little fairy waited and watched over her with an anxious heart.

On the morning of her sixteenth birthday Rosebud woke up feeling strangely restless. She wandered from room to room, and soon found herself in a part of the palace she had never seen before. Excitedly, she climbed faster and faster up the steps of an old tower until she reached a door at the top. It opened at the lightest touch and there in front of her was a little old woman working at a spinning wheel.

Rosebud had never seen a spindle before and it seemed like magic. "What are you doing?" she asked. "Can I try?"

"If you like," smiled the old woman, taking Rosebud's hand. "Here you are!"

But as soon as Rosebud touched the spindle, the sharp needle pricked her finger and she fell at once to the ground in a deep sleep.

"See! You can't escape from my spell!" hissed the old lady, for she was Malevola in disguise. And then, triumphantly, she slipped away.

Luckily the little fairy was already searching for the Princess and, warning the King and Queen, hurried to the tower. There they found Rosebud fast asleep by the spinning wheel.

All day they wept and called her name, gently touching her face and rubbing her hands, but it was no use. Rosebud remained asleep, smiling prettily as though dreaming.

At last with a heavy heart the King carried Rosebud to her room, and laid her on her bed.

Then it was time for the little fairy to carry out what she had been planning ever since Malevola cast her evil spell. Gently, she touched the King and Queen, who yawned and soon sank quietly into a deep sleep.

One by one, the fairy touched the cooks and the courtiers, the pages and the maids, until the whole palace was quiet except for the sound of gentle breathing. Even the cats and dogs slept, the mice in the corn and the doves in the hayloft.

Outside in the gardens the wild roses quickly began to grow and huge briars covered the walls of the palace. Days passed, weeks, months and then years. Still the palace slept deep in enchantment, encircled by a forest of wild roses.

In the outside world, a legend grew up of a princess cursed by a wicked fairy. Everyone agreed that there were great treasures to be found in her palace, but that it was unlucky to go near. Some, braver than the rest, tried to hack through the briars. But at every stroke of their swords, the thorns grew back thicker than ever until, scratched and bleeding, they gave up and slunk back home.

Almost a hundred years had passed when a young prince, whose name was Florizel, went out riding in the forest. He soon became separated from his friends and had no idea where he was until, with growing excitement, he saw that he must be near the enchanted palace of the legend. Through the trees was a vast wall of wild roses and their scent flowed around him like honey, drawing him nearer.

He jumped down from his horse and raised his sword, ready to fight his way through.

But to Florizel's amazement, the thorns melted away and the roses parted in front of him.

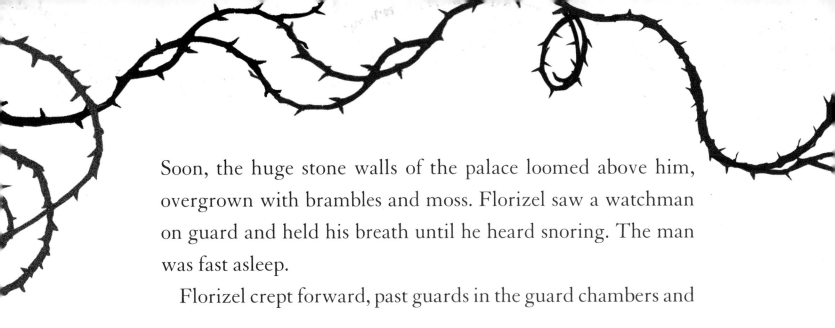

Soon, the huge stone walls of the palace loomed above him, overgrown with brambles and moss. Florizel saw a watchman on guard and held his breath until he heard snoring. The man was fast asleep.

Florizel crept forward, past guards in the guard chambers and

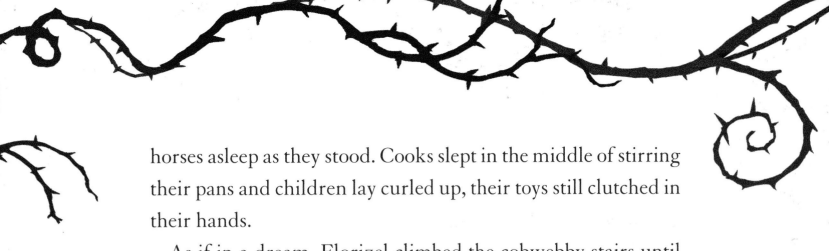

horses asleep as they stood. Cooks slept in the middle of stirring their pans and children lay curled up, their toys still clutched in their hands.

As if in a dream, Florizel climbed the cobwebby stairs until he came to a door and pushed it open…

The most beautiful princess he had ever seen lay on the bed asleep. Florizel leaned forward and kissed her hand, and her eyes fluttered and opened.

"My prince!" she said sweetly. "I have been dreaming about you. I knew you would come!"

And before they knew it, the Prince and Rosebud were talking and laughing as if they had known each other all their lives.

Meanwhile, the palace had also woken up and everyone was getting on with whatever they had been doing when they went to sleep. The dogs were chasing the cats, the sparrows were pecking at crumbs, the stable boy was leading out the horses and the cooks were starting to get the kitchens ready for supper.

The King and Queen soon discovered that the spell on their daughter had been broken and they wept tears of joy.

Not long after, it was announced that Prince Florizel and Princess Rosebud were to be married.

Everyone in the kingdom was invited to their magnificent wedding in the palace rose garden.

Rosebud wore an exquisite silk wedding dress and as she walked by, fairies showered her with fragrant petals.

Never had she looked more beautiful than when she looked into the eyes of her handsome prince and, smiling, each said, "I do."

It was the happiest day of their lives and the celebrations lasted well into the night.

The Prince and Princess, who became known as Sleeping Beauty, lived happily ever after, forever grateful for the magic of the little fairy.